Fred and Ted were friends.

Ted was small.

Fred was tall.

They were going on a trip.

Fred put a new part

on his green airplane.

Ted checked the oil

in his red airplane.

Beginner Books are written in simple language especially for beginning readers. If your child can read these lines, then he or she will be able to read this Beginner Book.

This book comes from the home of
THE CAT IN THE HAT

Beginner Books
A DIVISION OF RANDOM HOUSE, INC.

For a list of some other Beginner Books, see the back endpaper.

I CAN READ IT ALL BY MYSELF

Beginner Books

All rights reserved. Published in the United States by Random House Children's Books, a division of Random House, Inc., New York. BEGINNER BOOKS, RANDOM HOUSE, and the Random House colophon are registered trademarks of Random House, Inc. THE CAT IN THE HAT logo ® and © Dr. Seuss Enterprises, L.P. 1957, renewed 1986. All rights reserved.

www.randomhouse.com/kids

Educators and librarians, for a variety of teaching tools, visit us at
www.randomhouse.com/teachers

Library of Congress Cataloging-in-Publication Data
Eastman, Peter.
Fred and Ted like to fly / by Peter Eastman. — 1st ed.
    p. cm.
SUMMARY: Friends Fred and Ted fly their planes to the beach and enjoy spending the day together, even though they do things very differently all along the way.
ISBN 978-0-375-84064-7 (trade) — ISBN 978-0-375-94064-4 (lib. bdg.)
[1. Beaches—Fiction. 2. Airplanes—Fiction. 3. Individuality—Fiction.] I. Title.
PZ7.E13153Frl 2007 [E]—dc22 2006015444
Printed in the United States of America
10 9 8 7 6 5
First Edition

Fred and Ted Like to Fly

by Peter Eastman

BEGINNER BOOKS®

A Division of Random House, Inc.

Fred and Ted were friends.

Ted was small.

Fred was tall.

They were going on a trip.

Fred put a new part
on his green airplane.

Ted checked the oil
in his red airplane.

Fred pushed his airplane
onto the runway.

Ted pulled his airplane
onto the runway.

Fred stepped into his green airplane.

Ted jumped into his red airplane.

Fred flew right-side up.

Ted flew upside down.

Fred saw a good place to land.

Ted saw a better place to land.

Ted landed down on the sand.
Sand! Sand! Everywhere!

Fred landed
up on a tree!

They sat on the beach.

Ted was in the shade.

Fred was in the sun.

They went surfing.

Ted used a long board.

Fred used a short board.

When they reached the shore,

Ted fell down.

Fred stayed up.

They made sand castles.

Fred made a small one.

Ted made a big one.

They went for a walk.

Fred found a green shell.

Ted found a red shell.

Fred heard the ocean in his shell.

Ted heard a crab in his shell!

They played volleyball.

Ted hit the ball.

Fred missed
the ball.

They swam under water.

Fred saw a green fish.

Ted saw a red fish.

And then a little bird dove into the water!

CHEEP! CHEEP! it chirped.

The tide was coming in.
Water! Water! Everywhere!

Ted ran to his airplane on the sand.

Fred ran to his airplane on the tree.

They flew up high, over the water.

It was time to fly home.

Peter Eastman is the son of P. D. Eastman (1909–1986), author/illustrator of *Are You My Mother?*, *Go, Dog. Go!*, *The Best Nest*, and many other beloved children's books.

Peter followed his father into the animation field, working as an award-winning animator/director. *Fred and Ted Like to Fly* is his second book featuring the characters Fred and Ted.

Have you read
these all-time favorite
Beginner Books?

ARE YOU MY MOTHER?
by P. D. Eastman

THE BEST NEST
by P. D. Eastman

BIG DOG . . . LITTLE DOG
by P. D. Eastman

THE CAT IN THE HAT
by Dr. Seuss

FLAP YOUR WINGS
by P. D. Eastman

GO, DOG. GO!
by P. D. Eastman

FRED AND TED GO CAMPING
by Peter Eastman

SAM AND THE FIREFLY
by P. D. Eastman